Apollo Wept

Overture

Christopher "Coyote" Choate

Table of Contents

Copyright

Apollo Wept: Overture
Copyright © 2025 Christopher "Coyote" Choate
(Defiance Press & Publishing, LLC)

Published by Defiance Press & Publishing, LLC
Bulk orders of this book may be obtained by contacting Defiance Press & Publishing, LLC. www.defiancepress.com.
Defiance Press & Publishing, LLC
281-581-9300
info@defiancepress.com

Prelude

Legend says Alexander cried the day there were no more lands to conquer. When the engines of his beloved F-61 Mustang II spool down for the final time, Pen "Duke" Lencoln, America's last fighter pilot and leading ace from the conflict with China, understands the plight of the fabled Greek general all too well.

His career with the U.S. Aerospace Force is over. A premature conclusion, forced by the "Declaration of Guilt" signed by the President of "New America" and the subsequent dismantling of the military that once defended liberty across the globe. With few options remaining, Pen joins the U.S. Space Equity Collective—the last vestige of America's once-proud armed forces.

The former combat pilot now shuttles the nation's privileged elite between Earth and the lunar colonies, resigned to his fate as little more than a glorified bus driver. But destiny has other plans when a government-mandated purge of twentieth century archives unearths the ancient Voyager probe, launched during the "faux age" of the 1970s. Public outrage erupts when officials discover the probe carries a golden plaque depicting only male and female human forms—an artifact that fails to represent the federally recognized spectrum of gender identities. In the new social order, such "erasure" constitutes the highest crime: denial.

To Pen's astonishment, he is selected to oversee the USS DESPAIR, a Chinese-manufactured vessel tasked with intercepting Voyager beyond the solar system to replace the "offensive" plaque with a government-approved design acknowledging all 101 recognized genders and 68 sexual orientations. While agnostic to the purpose, Pen is completely dedicated to the task. But his commitment falters as he meets an elementary teacher in an illegal 1980 themed speak easy just weeks before leaving on his multi-year mission out of the solar system.

Unknown to Pen, powerful forces within both America and China are maneuvering to ensure his mission fails. But failure isn't in a fighter pilot's vocabulary. And with help from the Second Republic of Texas and a relative who died before Pen was born, he will lead his crew on humanity's most audacious undertaking yet. If Pen can beat the insurmountable odds stacked against him and do the impossible, he may even save Western Civilization from its self-inflicted demise.

Chapter One

Gahe Geronimo-Cortez
President of New America
Washingtin, Earth
August 5, 2096

"People, please, if you are still emotionally distressed, we have safe places in the adjoining room. I ask all of you too distraught to deal with the current situation to go now as the President will be joining us soon. But please remember to use your approved safe place, one that matches your current identified gender, sexual orientation, and color of skin," Zen Bio (intersex/cupiosexual/brown-light) declares from zir podium. The omni-media-verse influencers guilty of the high pitched wailing take advantage of the offer and leave the Sanger Press Room of Equity at the Indignity House. Zen still hears a few sniffles and cries, but nothing that requires another directive to those that remain. The time is now 2:01 Mohican Standard Time, meaning President Gahe Geronimo-Cortez (two-spirit/omnisexual/tan-light) won't arrive for at least three more minutes for the 2:00 briefing, as being on-time is an undisputed sign of cismale supremacy and a practice discarded years ago.

The three minute estimate is off by four. At 2:08, Gahe Geronimo-Cortez, the president of New America enters the round press room. Ze is wearing a long skirt and top made of a patchwork collection of red and black diamonds. Each diamond is paired with three other diamonds forming a larger multi-color one. The colors as well as the geometric shapes pierce the dull gray surroundings. This would be problematic for the president had the bright material not been the traditional clothing of the Seminole tribe. That's the president's ancestral family. Well, today at least. It was the Choctaw not that long ago. The teleprompters on both sides of the podium come to life as Geronimo-Cortez takes center stage. The president looks out at the nation's most important influencers, which is another way of saying the influencers that live and work in Washingtin, since the newly named capital city is all that really matters. Gahe can feel the tension that consumes the round room. This has been one of, if not the most, trying weeks in the eighteen years ze has been President of New America. Zir administration has focused all their effort on the president's three #1 top priorities (an example using the principles of equity math) to build the Great Society of Equity. The tens of trillions of yuan borrowed to achieve this utopia of social justice is now in jeopardy. Gahe Geronimo-Cortez knows this presentation will be the most important performance of zir political career. Even more important than when ze added nine Supreme Court Justices to ensure the Electoral College would be declared unconstitutional. The President places both hands across zir chest as a sign of peace and unity then warmly smiles as zir image is broadcast to a traumatized America. Many other nations are carrying the presentation as well, albeit for more comedic reasons. It's showtime.

"Good afternoon. I am here to discuss the horrifying news that has caused pain and suffering all across our stolen land. As you know, it was reported earlier this week that agents of the FBI-E made a shocking discovery as they were conducting a routine burning of records from the late twentieth century. The agent in charge of the purge observed a photo of a plaque on an ancient probe built by a racist and sexist organization known as the National Aeronautics and Space Administration. I want to commend this nonbinary-asexual-brown-dark agent. It could not have been easy to observe this offensive plaque; and it took an unwavering dedication to social justice to do what this agent did. Fortunately for humynkind, ze didn't hide this on a melting glacier. Ze did the equitable thing and reported the offense to our top social justice officials."

The president pauses and takes a small sip of water from an eco-friendly cup. Ze then continues, "Before we move forward, I want to warn my fellow triple-coded Americans that the following is disturbing. If you need to move to your safe place please do so now." After a short break the president resumes. "Based on the superb equitable work of our Space Equity Collective, we have determined that the probe in question was called Voyager and launched from Florida sometime during the 1970s. The probe or probes, we're not sure at the moment, travelled to the outer planets and departed the solar system early in this century. After reviewing all remaining records from this disturbing era, we have come to the conclusion that the probe does carry the plaque, and it is guilty of the highest of all crimes: denial. The false and disproven belief that nature only created two sexes."

A loud series of howls and moans fills the room. The stoic demeanor of several influencers falters, and they hurriedly exit the room as tears fall to the gray floor from their faces twisted in agony. Those remaining go silent as Secret Equity Service (SES) agents quickly enter the room. They have seen how the SES deals with people not complying with the directions given by the President. And none of them want to be on the receiving end of the attention.

"So let me clear, this probe is headed into the cosmos and will still be traveling through our galaxy long after we have turned our planet into a sizzling ball of inferno. This probe called Voyager will be our legacy. A bigoted legacy of denial. One that not only denies the many proud genders of our species, but implies cis as the only true sexual orientation. So once again, let me be perfectly clear. Our nation will pay the price, carry the burden, and meet whatever hardship is required to send a spaceship to intercept this horrific relic from our appalling past, and replace this plaque with a scientifically correct one showing all 101 genders and 68 sexual orientations. This will not only save our legacy, but will make the galaxy safe for social justice. And I will be contacting the General Secretary of China to discuss them building us a spaceship to make this happen. This will not stand!"

Chapter Two

Rene Smyth
Florida, Earth
October 16, 2103

"So how was your flight?"

I glance up from my glass of Moscato, the crystal rim catching the speakeasy's light as its reflected from a rotating ball in the ceiling. A man maybe ten years my junior stands before me, wrapped in what has to be the most peculiar suit I've ever seen – some impossible shade between peacock and midnight that ripples like liquid mercury. The fabric probably costs more than my monthly teacher's salary. Against his rich dark skin, the white shirt underneath actually works, though I'd never admit it aloud.

"I'm sorry?" I manage, genuinely puzzled.

"Your flight from Hollywood? You're an actor, right?"

I hide my eye roll behind a practiced smile. He's the fourth wannabe Romeo dispatched from what I've mentally dubbed the "Desperation Corner" – a table of increasingly bold suitors who've been working their way through what I now know is a greatest-hits collection of 1980s pickup lines. I discovered their playbook written on the "Cowgirls" bathroom wall, right between lipstick graffiti and phone numbers promising a good time. Apparently, there's a matching list in the men's room, though the ladies maintain a silent pact not to reveal this intel. Let them think they're being original.

"No, I'm not an actor – or actress, if we're being precise. Just a schoolteacher."

"A teacher?" His eyebrows shoot up as if I've just revealed I'm secretly a duchess. "Well, maybe I can have a seat and talk about me teaching you a few things tonight."

And we're done. The line itself is bad enough, but his wandering gaze makes it worse, treating what is below my neckline like it's hiding the answers to next week's lottery numbers. Yes, my dress is revealing – a nod to 1980s excess that I'd never wear outside this bar, one where I'm supposed to helping a friend celebrate her divorce from all five of her communal spouses. Who, along with our other friends, is currently at a "Free Love" establishment that I politely declined to visit. In Texas, we had a different name for those places, and I'll stick to my simple pleasures, thank you very much.

"Thanks, but I'm waiting for friends," I reply, my tone pleasant but my face suggesting he should find another classroom.

"I don't think you realize what you're missing," he says, his smile curdling into something ugly.

"Oh, I think I do," I counter, my stare cold enough to frost his overpriced suit.

"Your loss, bitch," he spits, retreating to his corner like a wounded peacock.

There's still one more contestant at their table. I silently pray he's more perceptive than his friends. I'm about to give up on my wayward companions – who promised to meet me here over an hour ago – when a shadow falls across my table. I ignore it at first, too engrossed in watching Tom Cruise's Maverick chase Kelly McGillis's Charlie around a bar, not unlike this one, on a large vintage screen above an image of an attractive lady named Farrah.

But the presence lingers, and I turn, ready to shut down another tired line – only to have the words die in my throat.

He stands there in an antiquated flight suit that looks anything but costume. Everything about him – from his commanding posture to the quiet confidence in his eyes – screams of a tactical aviator. The type that once flew remarkable machines that would break the sound barrier with ease. His smile is warm, genuine, reaching eyes that have seen the curve of the Earth from above. He's holding two drinks, one of which looks suspiciously like my preferred Moscato. He'll get extra credit if its Italian. But what catches me off guard is how he's studying the small tattoo on my shoulder with genuine curiosity rather than using it as an excuse to ogle.

He recovers smoothly from being caught staring, and in a voice that carries the authority of someone who was once a "master of the air:"

"Have you seen any MiGs lately?"

Despite myself, I feel the corners of my mouth tugging upward. Okay, flyboy. You have my attention.

Chapter Three

Pen "Duke" Lencoln
Florida, Earth
October 16, 2103

There it is. And right on time. The first glimmer of light emerges from the abyss, causing a faint view of the horizon to appear, as the pitch-black darkness is expelled by a deep metallic purple. Soon, this dark violet will fade, transforming into stunning shades of rich blue, followed by an array of warm yellow, burnt orange, and dazzling red.

I take a sip of my carbon neutral coffee as Apollo's chariot makes its appearance over the calm Atlantic Ocean. There's enough light now to see there isn't a cloud in the sky. Sweet. It's easy to take the beauty of a sunrise for granted. I've done it most of my life. But not now. My opportunities to witness this remarkable event are dwindling. Like many things in life, the beauty of the sunrise is lost in redundancy. That is until you can no longer take it for granted. I'm at that point. Sure, I should have this privilege again years from now. Should being the key word.

The darker shades of majestic colors disappear as the source of all life on Earth continues climbing above the eastern horizon. A wave of energy expands across my body as my skin absorbs the arriving heat, causing my prefrontal cortex to begin registering the multitude of tasks I need to be working. I consciously shutdown this effort at multi-tasking. I take another sip of coffee and recline the old patio chair back as the rust formed by the exposure to the sea air makes a grinding protest to the rotation of the mechanical joints. I consume the remaining moments of sunrise with a deliberate serenity, my mind void of all else.

Our middle-aged star clears the ocean as the calm of the crisp morning is broken by a series of audio tones informing me of messages arriving on my e-tab. Nature's show has made its final call, so I put my coffee on a cheap plastic table in the middle of my small patio, one I should have used more than I have. I rotate the zero-gravity chair to a more vertical position as I notice the first message is from my younger sister. She just landed in Tel Aviv on her flight that departed Orlando a few hours ago. It was our first visit in years, as she left America for Israel when she was informed her career advancement had peaked due to her identified gender, sexual orientation, and skin color categorization.

Her message is short and crisp. Typical for an engineer. The flight was short and smooth. No surprise for a craft travelling Mach 6 at 120,000 feet. Food was good enough. She finished the message repeating my line at the airport. One where I promised to visit her new home on my return from leaving the solar system. It's a promise I plan to keep, if I can. I've never been to Israel. I was within minutes of going once with my then squadron commander, "Tex" Riggins (yes, the one that is now the President of Texas). We were to speak to the Israeli National War College about our experience during the conflict with China. We were in our seats on the commercial flight at Dulles-Massasoit International when agents from the Federal Bureau of Investigation and Equity came onboard and escorted us off the jet. That was embarrassing as you can imagine. Turns out our employer, the now defunct U.S. Aerospace Force, didn't get permission for our trip. China found out and was not happy. They informed Washingtin of their displeasure and before you know it, America's first "ace" fighter pilots in over a century are being detained by their own government. I did try to visit her years later, but I didn't have enough carbon credits for the flight. I still don't even today. I reply to her message with the obligatory. It was great seeing you, thanks for flying over, I love you, and I will definitely visit on my return from space. I'll be gone long enough on this trip beyond the bonds of Earth that carbon credits shouldn't be a problem.

The second message is a reminder to watch a teleconference from Washingtin later today. President Gahe Geronimo-Cortez and Will

Borgmyn will be addressing our upcoming herstoric mission. Borgmyn will be the Senior Social Justice Officer of my ship. I was originally scheduled to be part of the teleconference, but my identified gender, sexual orientation and color of skin made that problematic. I've never been a fan of talking to the media influencers, so I really didn't care when I was told not to attend. Besides, with the President of New America and the most prominent social justice officer in our nation attending, there really isn't a need for the overseer (or "captain" as the clingers still call my position) of the ship to be present.

The next message is from an old college friend. We're meeting tonight for the first time in years at a speakeasy in Orlando. And yes, as the name implies, the club is illegal as it lacks any equitable purpose. But a lot of things are not legal these days, so I'm not really concerned. Besides, it could be fun. The bar is themed after the 1980s, complete with something called music videos and numerous movies from that era being projected from vintage screens mounted along the walls. Tim and I will be wearing antiquated flight suits of U.S. Naval Aviators. They have something to do with a popular movie from that decade. The olive-green coveralls look like my old USAF flight suit but flashier for lack of a better word. The patches on the uniform represent a squadron designated as VF-1. They flew a jet called the "Tomcat" as several of the patches have images of that swing-wing fighter. The jet is definitely an antique compared to the F-61 Mustang II I used to fly, but it looks like an impressive machine nonetheless. The left shoulder is adorned with the red, white, and blue flag of Old America. That could be a problem if we're seen wearing it by the wrong people. That won't an issue at the speakeasy. Or so I was told.

I scroll through the message and discover we won't be meeting tonight after all. Tim works for the Climate Crisis Action Team and has an important briefing to give on Monday. It's an assessment of the Florida shoreline 200 years from now and his team will have to work all weekend to have it ready. You would think they could slip the briefing since it deals with something happening over two centuries from now, but, like me, he works for the U.S. government. Meetings are sanctimonious events in our world and cancelling one takes the proverbial executive order. That ain't happening. I decide not to go, but before I finish the message Tim is adamant that I attend. Getting an invite to this distinctive club is not easy and if both of us are no shows, he will lose out on future invites. So, it looks like I'll be alone and unafraid as I meet at the assigned arrival point. When I arrive at the secret location, my code words are "Vader. Darth Vader." I'm not sure who, or what that is. From there I'll be given the instructions to the speakeasy known as Polys. My expectations have nose-dived since I'll be solo and without a clue on the club. But I'm an optimist, I'll make the best of it. And since my time remaining on Earth is down to weeks, I have no intention of looking for any type of relationship that goes beyond a single night. Well, maybe two or three, four max. Like we said in my fighter squadron years ago, "it depends."

Chapter Four

William "Tex" Riggins
Commander, 90th Fighter Squadron
Andersen Aerospace Base, Guam, Earth
March 23, 2087

"Dice check main."

"Two." "Three." "Four."

"Vegas check."

"Two." "Three. Need two mike, INS." "Four."

"Reno."

"Two." "Three."

"Andersen Ground, Dice flight with Vegas and Reno on 257.8, unable data-comm."

"Dice 01, Andersen ground, data-comm is tango-uniform. We'll be voice all day. Hold position, still awaiting clearance."

"Dice 01 copy," I reply with a dry and unemotional tone. My radio call doesn't reflect it, but I'm eager to get my jets off this volcanic rock and back home to Alaska. I say eager, desperate is more accurate. Too much is going too wrong too fast. It's been three days since I led 16 Mustangs from Elmendorf-Aleut Aerospace Base south to defend Guam from an impending attack by the combined forces of the People's Republic of China. The air battle against a larger Chinese force was fierce, but went much better than I expected had I been honest with my pilots. (I wasn't if you're wondering). I did lose five F-61 Mustangs and tragically, three pilots. But I expected the losses to be much worse. By skill or luck, we were able to catch the Chinese fighters by surprise which made the difference in the outcome. The sacrifice made by my pilots combined with the heroic efforts of a small group of Marines turned the tide, and prevented Guam from becoming another beach front property of the communist government of China, as well as a strategic outpost in the middle of the Pacific. And I should thank the U.S. Navy. The attack subs USS SACRAMENTO and USS SAN ANTONIO left all three of China's formidable super carriers dead in the water, putting an end to their plan for additional real estate.

The euphoria of our unexpected victory was short lived. I would explain why, if I had a clue what happened. The calendar hadn't turned to the next day when the media was reporting that officials in Washingtin were apologizing to China and accusing the U.S. military of taken action that was never approved by the president. It went downhill from there. Enough so that I begged the 11th Air Force Commander to send three unmanned air refueling drones from Alaska to Guam so we could get the hell outta Dodge.

"Dice 1, ground. Your squadron ops is requesting you contact them on 303.0 secure."

This can't be good. "Dice 01 will do. Dice-Vegas-Reno, push 303.0 secure on aux." I give my pilots a moment to set up the secure comm on their aux radios. "Dice deployed, Dice 01," I say, my voice a deep hollow from the circuits that scramble the radio transmission.

"Tex, this is BACH. What's your status?"

"Still in the chocks. Awaiting clearance."

"Tex here's the SITREP," my assistant director of operations replies with a choppy and rapid reply. It's nothing like his normal voice, one that drops the 'R' and rounds 'O,' courtesy of him spending his formative years along the rocky coastline of Rhode Island. "I'm locked in our ops vault. Agents with the FBI-E are crawling all over the place. They're confiscating our computers and giving everyone a gag order telling us we'll be arrested if we discuss anything related to the ops against China."

My stomach knots with BACH's words. I want to ask a dozen questions but my training prohibits me from asking.

He continues. "I've tried to contact home base with no luck. The media is reporting that Admiral McCluskey in Hawaii has been detained. There's a picture of her being taken to an FBI-E van in handcuffs, but it's been removed from the omni-media-verse."

The knots expand across my body with that piece of information. Admiral McCluskey is the commander of Pacific Command. She was the one that authorized my squadron to engage the Chinese forces. She would have received her authorization from the Secretary of Defense and Equity. I have no idea what's happening at this point, but I easily surmise the CYA game is in full swing back in Washingtin.

"Copy all BACH," I answer fighting to keep my voice calm and void of emotion. "What's your status?"

"I'm in the ops vault. I changed the combo to the vault and had admin lock me in. The FBI-E won't be entering here for some time. That said boss, I recommend you takeoff ASAP. I suspect they have already cancelled your flight clearance."

I was thinking the same. "Copy BACH. I'll launch the unmanned tankers and we'll depart VFR."

"Copy boss. I'll maintain this frequency. I'll see if I can delay the FBI-E from here."

I call up the unmanned tanker command page on my multi-function display. I have the AI system plot our flight back to Alaska and the fuel required. We're good.

"Ground, Dice 01. What's the ETIC on our clearance," I ask across the main radio.

I'm answered with static so I repeat the question.

"Lieutenant Colonel Riggins, this is Bell Joy, senior agent with the FBI-E. You and your pilots are hereby ordered to shut down your engines immediately and exit the aircraft."

Like hell I will. "Andersen ground, please reply you were stepped on," I answer on the main radio. I then direct our unmanned aerial tankers to taxi to runway 7 Right for an immediate takeoff.

"I said shutdown your engines and exit the aircraft. Failure to do so and you will be charged with numerous felonies. Am I clear?"

I key the main radio, "Ground, you're now coming in broken and stupid. Please repeat." I immediately switch to the aux. "Dicemen, on my authority, quick taxi to runway 7, alternate takeoffs using both runways. Full afterburner climb to 17,000 feet and maintain one mile radar trail." Vegas and Reno flight leads crisply acknowledge my command as I start my faster than normal taxi down the center taxiway.

I taxi past the oversized concrete pads that once hosted the massive B-52 bomber. The crews of those bombers tried in vain to win a war their inept leadership back in Washingtin had no intention of winning. I can't help but wonder what they would think of the actions taking by our government today. The roar of the hybrid-ramjet engines on the KQ-25 brings me back to the task at hand as the unmanned aircraft accelerates down the runway. I'm watching the second tanker take the runway when BACH comes across the aux radio.

"Tex – they are putting fire trucks on the runways. You need to hurry!"

"Copy," I reply. I look over left shoulder and see the doors to the fire station opening. I do a quick bit of algebra, similar to the problem we learned in school, one where an electric car leaves point A at 20 mph and a planet killing gas burning car leaves point B at 60 mph. I decide I can get airborne, but it could be problematic for the jets behind me.

The last tanker lifts off after a takeoff roll off 7,000 feet. The first fire truck takes the runway as the drone goes airborne and raises its gear. If I had time, I might be able to come up with a better plan. But I don't.

"Duke, proceed to 7 left. Takeoff if you have the one thousand feet needed. If a truck is on the runway jettison every flare you have on him."

"Copy," America's leading ace with eight aerial victories replies, three more than me by the way. I make the turn onto runway 7 right and push the throttles into maximum afterburner once I'm aligned with the runway. My Mustang responds providing 90,000 pounds of thrust throwing me back hard into the seat. That never gets old. The truck is still 5,000 feet away. I'm violating a number of safety regulations but I've got plenty of runway to takeoff. I raise the gear as the jet rapidly accelerates and "slips the surly bonds of Earth." I level off twenty feet above the deck and arm the flares I'm carrying. They are designed to counter heat seeking missiles, but they'll do just fine for the task at hand. I set the dispenser to emergency – that will eject all 80 of them simultaneously. As I rapidly approach the fire truck in our pickup game of chicken, it becomes apparent the driver is not too excited to the task he has been given by the agents of the FBI-E. I see the truck slow down and check to the right. Smart move on his or her part. I jettison the flares early sending a massive display of fireworks out the tail of my jet as the flares bounce off the asphalt spraying sparks across the width of the runway. The pyrotechnics cause the driver to swerve violently sending the top-heavy truck to its side as it slides off the runway. As I pass the disabled truck I look to the other runway and see Duke using the same plan of attack. The driver approaching him is either more dedicated or not as smart. His devotion or stupidity results in his truck being engulfed by the burning flares, blowing every tire and causing fires to break out behind the cab. The truck departs the north side of the runway as the driver and suspected FBI-E agent jump from the burning vehicle. I would love to hear the debrief of their plan. I'm sure it'll be entertaining.

"7 Left is good for takeoff. You've got over 5,000 feet available," Dice 03 informs my flight.

I turn to the north as I get radar contact on the tankers that are headed to the state once known as "The Last Frontier." I disconnect my oxygen mask and rub my hand across my face once my last jet is airborne. My hand is covered in sweat. I engage the autopilot and take a small water bottle from my g-suit pocket. With my adrenaline returning to its normal range, my mind immediately moves to what's next. I wish I knew. I can't believe things have to come this. I have no idea what happens once we land in Alaska. I was lawyer before I joined the Air Force. The education I received at the University of Texas Law School tells me to expect the worse, and this is probably my last flight in a Mustang. The corners of my mouth drop with that thought. The lawyer in me says I was following the lawful orders given to me by my superior officer. The average American citizen side of me knows how well that will go. You know, going back to Texas and practicing law can't be that bad. Who knows, I might even run for governor.

Chapter Five

Antonio "Cherry" Washingtin
Florida, Earth
May 7, 2088

Sure, you can call me Cherry. But be careful who's around when you say it. It's my callsign. That makes it a violation of military regulations, as well as a Presidential executive order (EO). I don't remember the exact number, but it's the EO banning toxic masculinity. The same one that outlawed whiskey and other liquors determined by a collaboration of government agencies to be "masculine" in nature. Important work by America's best and brightest, no doubt.

Since you asked, I can give you some of the background on how I "earned" the name. To start with, it was given to me at a naming ceremony about two months ago. I was a student F-61 pilot with the 58th Fighter Squadron, a unit with a distinctive history dating back to the Racist World War in the mid-20th Century (that's the war that ended with our criminal use of nuclear weapons). It's not easy to explain a naming ceremony, it's something you have to experience firsthand. Which is not easy since it's a closed event. It was like that even before they became illegal. For me, I was in front of the F-61 instructors and my fellow student pilots in the dimly lit squadron heritage and equity room (aka a bar). An oversized image of a large gorilla with red eyes and long imposing fangs was hanging from the wall behind me. "58th Fighter Squadron – The Mighty Gorillas" was written in bold red letters along the bottom with ten silhouettes of enemy aircraft ranging from the Mig-29 Fulcrum of the old Soviet Union to the Messerschmitt-109 of Nazi Germany. All victims of the squadron pilots who came before me. Without question, the artwork is a prohibited relic from the "faux" era of Old America. The instructors didn't say where they hide it; and I didn't ask. Beside me on a makeshift stage is my primary instructor pilot, Captain "Duke" Lencoln. He's America's leading ace, with eight aerial victories from the misunderstanding with China just over a year prior. He is giving a lecture to the fraternity of aviators on my exploits in the F-61. Some of it is true, about ten percent, I would guess. The rest is a highly inflated dialogue of the mistakes I've made during my training. The instructors howl with each example. Duke's performance is entertaining, but I suspect the massive amount of alcohol consumed by his audience has more to do with the booming laughter than the quality of his jokes. Anyway, the name Cherry came from his presentation. It has something to do with my last name (which was once spelled "Washington." My ancestors replaced the "o" with an "i" around the time our nation's capital did the same). His tale about lying your ass off when caught with an axe didn't make much sense to me. The older instructor pilots thought it was hilarious. They remember Old America. I on the other hand, do not.

All that occurred in the building I'm now standing in. Not quite three weeks ago, the "Creech Brown" stucco building that hosted the unit formerly known as the gorillas was bristling with activity. Pilots would be standing at the ops desk, weighted down with over fifty pounds of flight gear, to receive the latest status on the condition of the airfield and the jets they were about to take into the heavens; a senior maintenance troop would be in a heated discussion with the squadron's director of operations about something. The subject didn't matter, the conversation was always loud with lots of hand waving and rolling of eyes. Profanity was expected, probably even encouraged, but they would always end with a handshake. Well, it would as long as no one from outside the squadron was around to see it. Those days are gone. Right after the announcement was made that we had signed the statement of guilt concerning our actions against China over Guam, our squadron commander called a meeting and informed us our flying operations would cease immediately. The details came about two days later. It turns out the president signed more than just a statement of guilt. We also received a significant increase in Chinese funding for our national budget. While that bit of good news was cheered from one coast of our stolen land to the other, not everyone was ecstatic about the Chinese rescuing us from our latest budget crisis. Specifically, those of us in the military. We were toast. Part of the agreement disbanded our entire force of "personned" fighter aircraft. I had just graduated from the F-61 training and was within days of leaving Eglin-Obama Aerospace Base for my operational assignment in New Mexico. Not now. Today, I must figure out what to do since my career as a USAF fighter pilot was over before it even started.

I walked down the dark and empty hallway still marked with pictures of the fighter aircraft that made the USAF the world's premier air force for over a century. I'm the only person in the building when I exit the doors leading to the flightline. Once outside in the oppressive Florida air, the experience becomes more surreal than it already is. There's not a sound to be heard. Nothing. Our twenty-four F-61 Mustang II fighters set underneath their weather shelters motionless. Normally, at this time of day, eight of them would be preparing to takeoff, their massive engines shattering the calm with a high-pitched scream informing everyone around they were ready to rule the skies. Sadly, those days are no more. The proud birds will take to the air once more as they are sent to Arizona, where they will be dismantled and scrapped. Not much different than me I'm afraid.

"What are you doing here?" The question breaks the silence and my current bout of self-pity. I turn around to see America's leading ace looking at me with raised eyebrows. You would never know he's our, well was, top fighter pilot. He's wearing a pair of ragged shorts, and a collarless short sleeve shirt covered with a mismatch of palm trees and tropical birds of every make and model. It's something the tourists wear when they visit Florida in the summer. For us locals, we wouldn't be caught dead in a shirt like that. Most of us that is. At least his sunglasses look the part of being an elite fighter pilot.

"Hey Duke, that's a good question. I'm not sure. I guess I wanted to see our jets one more time before we melt them into low-alcohol beer cans."

My former instructor pilot nods and walks up slowly beside me. He doesn't say it, but I believe he's here for the same reason. "Have you started looking for a new career?" he asks.

I sigh. "Not really. I guess I'm still in the denial phase."

Pen answers with a small and twisted smile. "Understandable."

"How about you? What are you going to do?"

"I've been offered a position with the Space Equity Collective. Apparently, they'll let me pilot a shuttle between the Moon and Earth," he replies frowning. "I've been to space a half dozen times or so, gotta say I'm not a fan. I much rather stay within the atmosphere."

"Well. At least you'll be flying something."

"True," Duke replies. "What are thinking?"

"No idea," I quickly, and honestly, answer.

"Would you consider joining me? I have a contact in the Space Equity Collective Headquarters. She has a lot of clout, and she owes me one on top of that."

Space. I never had any real desire to work in space, just like Duke. But what I've wanted to do since I was a young boy in Lower Illinois (don't call it Southern) is no longer an option. I give it a moment of thought before replying, "That's interesting. Can I think about it?"

"Sure. I still have several weeks before reporting. I just found out I'll be leading the last four ship of Mustangs to the boneyard," Duke replies as a bitter expression moves across his face.

I give him a slight nod before saying, "Congrats, looks like you'll be America's last fighter pilot."

Chapter Six

Dr. William R. "Pop" Lincoln
Illinois, Earth
March 24, 2056

Don't panic. I keep telling myself that. But I always return to that primal instinct. And for good reason. Nothing makes sense. I'm in some type of fog, yet, my mind is perfectly clear. In fact, time seems to be moving slower than normal as my mental faculties are crisp and razor sharp. That's not helping because I feel nothing. My brain is void of any sensory perception. Sight, touch, sound, are all empty like I'm in the deepest pit of hell. My first thought was I had suffered a stroke, but I quickly realized my mind is much too clear for me to have succumbed to that tragic event. My next assumption is I've been in a terrible accident, one that has left me unimpaired mentally, but paralyzed from my body. I went mad with that thought, my mind reacting like I was just buried alive. Fortunately, I was able to regain some control over my darkest fears. Had I not done so, I'm afraid I spend the rest of my time, however long or short that is, in a horrid abyss of despair. I'm trying to recover my short-term memory when I hear a voice that sounds familiar. I can't quite understand it at first, but it seems to be getting clearer.

"Doctor Lincoln, can you hear me?" I finally grasp on the fourth attempt.

"Yes! I can! Where am I? What's happened to me?" I frantically reply, unsure of how I did.

"Doctor, you're fine. All this is temporary. I will explain, but first, can you tell me the last thing you remember?"

I'm fine? Really? Easy for this a-hole to say. And the last thing I remember? I'm not sure. What a minute. It's coming to me. "There was a presidential election. The winner was, uh, Trump. Donald Trump."

"Good. Was it his first or second time?"

"I only remember one," I reply. "Was there a second?"

"That's good," the still unidentified voice replies. "Do you remember anything personal or work related?"

I focus my mental acuity on the question. All of sudden, its right there. "Yes, I work at MIT. We're working on artificial intelligence."

"How about your family?" the familiar but unnamed voice asks.

"I'm married with two children. Both grown." My mind becomes overwrought as I realize why I recognize the voice. It's the voice of my son. "Kurt, is that you?"

————-

"Okay, I've paused the program," Kurt Lincoln says to the elderly man beside him. The younger Dr. Lincoln smiles as he watches the tears flow down the age lines of his father. "Does that sound like you?"

The elder Dr. Lincoln pulls a small handkerchief out of the breast pocket of his dated polo shirt. He dries the small tears from his face then uses the dry part of the cloth to clean his glasses. Time has taken its toll on the brilliant computer scientist, but not so much that he didn't understand the dilemma his son was facing. "Yes, it does," he answers carefully. "But you realize that isn't me? It's my memories and my intellectual traits, yes, but, you are dealing with an intelligence built on silicon and replicas of human neurons. One with free will and the capacity to make independent decisions. You're going to have to find a way to explain to him what we have built and see if he wants to be part of this. He may not relish the thought of being a digital entity without a physical body."

The younger Dr. Lincoln purses his lips as he slowly nods his head. "I do Pop. I didn't really at first, but I've come to that conclusion. If I don't handle the bootup right, this may all be for naught."

The old man slowly stands up, pushing on both thighs to help his weakening leg muscles overcome the weight of his body. He stiffly walks to his son and puts his arm around his shoulder. With a smile of an admiration, he looks at his son as he sees both him and his late wife in their older child. Another small tear flows from his aging eyes that are still sharp and vivid, despite the many decades he has spent on Earth. He takes a deep breath to ensure his voice won't crack under the emotions that are overwhelming him and says, "Son, you'll figure it out. I know you will. You're the brightest computer scientist I ever worked with, and you have your Mom's drive and perseverance. That combination can do the impossible."

Chapter Seven

Will Borgmyn
Washingtin, Earth
June 20, 2102

"We are live in three, two, one."

"Greetings my fellow triple-coded Americans and everyone fortunate enough to live beyond the borders of this stained nation. I am Flower Dignity and this is 'America the Shameful,' the most watched omni-media-cast in all of our stolen land" the agender-metrosexual-black-light influencer says with a warm smile. The American celebrity is sitting behind a plain gray desk of which only half is visible. Ze is wearing a customary gray one piece garment. A small eco-friendly necklace adorned with the required 169 colors is just long enough to reach the top of the dull fabric. Behind Flower in zir studio on the curved gray wall is an oversized photo of several planet-killing construction machines billowing black smoke from their evil internal combustion engines. A sign proudly announcing the project as the "Hoover Dam" is visible on the far left of the non-color image. The dam was one of the original "seven white cismale sins of America" when the list was announced in 2042. Today, it is only one remaining, the carbon footprint of removing the massive concrete structure being too high for the nation to pay, as it would jeopardize New America's treasured zero-carbon footprint rating. So the evil work of engineering remains, it and the nearly dry Colorado river being a national herstoric site of remorse. Flower continues, "Today, we have a BANNER omni-cast for you," zir body twitching with excitement. The video that is being sent all across Earth and the stations on the moon and Mars then expands outward to show the source of zir excitement. "With me today is America's most equitable influencer, no other than Will Borgmyn!"

Will looks at the camera with zis trademark lowered lips and focused eyebrows. The prominent social justice influencer then turns to Flower: "Thank you. I'm glad to be here. I do wish things were better but, that's just the turbulent times we live in as we continue to pay for the shortfalls of our bigoted founders."

Flower's demeanor turns pale as Will speaks. "That is so true, so true," ze adds as small tears pool on the corners of zir eye." Flower wipes the tears away and takes a deep breath. "I guess we should start with the most obvious question of the day: what is your take on a cismale-heterosexual-white being assigned as the overseer of the USS DESPAIR?

A trigger warning flashes across the video feed as Will massages zis chin with zis hand. Ze pauses before answering. "As you know Flower, I am a Tier One Social Justice Officer with the U.S. government. I have dedicated my life to promoting social justice and the pillars of diversity, inclusion, and equity."

"Absolutely!" Flower fawns.

"To be honest, I was shocked like all Americans. DESPAIR will undertake the most important mission ever attempted by humynkind. The thought of DESPAIR failing to remove the horrible plaque from that bigoted probe is beyond comprehension," Borgmyn says in anguish. The nation's most prominent warrior of social justice then turns to look straight into the camera. "It's like education. We know education is too important to leave to the parents. Well, I believe a social justice offense of this magnitude is too important to leave to a cismale-heterosexual-white. So yes, I felt ill after hearing the announcement and went to my safe place for several hours until I could regain my composure."

"Do you know this white cismale, uh, Lencoln I believe?"

"I don't," Borgmyn replies. "I know ze was a former fighter pilot. That's not comforting either."

"Definitely," Flower answers. Ze then leans forward towards the gray table and asks, "can you tell us what the Indignity House was thinking by assigning a straight white male as overseer? It just seems unimaginable that President Gahe Geronimo-Cortez (two-spirit/omnisexual/tan-light) would make that decision."

"Ze didn't," Borgmyn answers. "I spoke with the President the next day and ze assured me that decision was made by the U.S. Space Equity Collective."

Flower sighs in relief. "Well, that's good to hear. Did you tell the President of your concern?"

"I did," Borgmyn replies with a raised chin. "I said that I was gravely concerned and offered my services."

"In what way?"

"I volunteered to be the social justice officer on DESPAIR," Borgmyn replies.

"No way!" Flower gushes.

"I did. And the President enthusiastically accepted."

Flower's eyes explode with Borgmyn's proclamation. "This is so wonderful! Just to be clear, you are saying that Will Borgmyn, America's most prominent official of social justice, will be the social justice officer on USS DESPAIR when our Chinese-built spaceship leaves Earth to replace the disgusting plague on the bigoted Voyager probe?"

"That's correct."

Flower's face is beaming as ze bounces with excitement. "I'm almost speechless. And relieved. I know I speak for all the people in our tainted nation, when I say it's such a relief to know that you will be on DESPAIR, in the most important position on the ship, as it leaves the solar system to save the legacy of humynkind from our stained ancestors."

"That's very equitable of you, Flower. But it was an easy decision. As America has heard me say on many occasions, I have devoted my life to the belief in equity today, equity tomorrow, and equity forever!"

Read On!

Look for Apollo Wept: A Space Opera Trilogy by Christopher "Coyote" Choate coming soon from Defiance Press. It will be available in audio, eBook, and paperback everywhere you buy books!